Prince

AND THE CASE OF THE

Smelly Goat

Also available in Hodder Story Books

Prince Vince and the
Hot Diggory Dogs

Text copyright © Valerie Wilding 1995
Illustrations copyright © Guy Parker-Rees 1995

First published in Great Britain in 1995
by Hodder Children's Books

10   9   8   7   6   5   4   3   2   1

A Catalogue record for this book is available from the British Library

ISBN 0340 626534

Printed and bound in Great Britain by
Cox & Wyman Ltd, Reading, Berks.

Hodder Children's Books
A Division of Hodder Headline plc
338 Euston Road
London NW1 3BH

Prince Vince

AND THE CASE OF THE

Smelly Goat

BY VALERIE WILDING

ILLUSTRATED BY GUY PARKER-REES

Hodder
Children's
Books

a division of Hodder Headline plc

For my father
Donald Charles Allin
with love.

1

KIDNAP

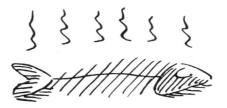

On Wednesday, Macclesfield the butler said an unbelievably rude word in front of the Royal Family.

The Queen's spoon dripped porridge on her book of ghost stories and the King clapped his hands over his son's ears. That wasn't easy. His son was considerably taller than he was, even sitting down.

Prince Vincent Alexandro de Maximus Roy, better known as Prince Vince, pulled free. "I'm not a kid any more, Dad," he said. "One swear word won't hurt. What's it mean, Macclesfield?"

"It means, Your Highness," said the butler, between sucks of his thumb, "that I've cut myself again."

The Queen sighed. "Pass him your napkin, Vince. Quick, before he bleeds to *death*."

Prince Vince sprang up but, instead of a napkin, he grabbed the tablecloth. Swish! Crash! Half the Royal breakfast shot to the floor. Unfortunately, the other end of the cloth was tucked into the King's collar. The force of Vince's pull jerked him so hard he bashed his forehead on the table and lost his false tooth in the scrambled eggs.

"Ow!" he roared, but the others were absorbed in mopping up Macclesfield. "Ow, everyone!" He gave up and poked about in the scrambled eggs until he found his tooth, grumbling non-stop. "Stupid boy. Calls himself grown up, does he? Wants a proper job?" He found the tooth, sucked it clean and popped it into place. "Fat chance. Takes me all my time training him to be King."

Macclesfield, recovered from his tenth cut since Christmas, ordered a footman to clear up the mess.

He'd barely begun when Captain Boxer of the King's Guard appeared, standing to attention in the doorway, tufty moustache awry and nose aimed at the ceiling.

"Beg pardon for distarbin' the Royal porridge, Yer Maje*sty*, Yer Majesty *Ma'am*, Yer 'ighness."

The Queen sighed and closed her book.

"Come in, Boxer," said the King.

"*Sah!*" Captain Boxer stamped twice and marched forward, nose so high he didn't see the footman, crawling round with dustpan and brush, until too late.

Prince Vince, learning a second swear word that morning, helped Captain Boxer up and peeled a bacon rasher from his jacket. The Queen dragged a chair to the window and buried her nose in her book. The King sucked his tooth and let the Captain collect his wits.

"Beg pardon, Yer Majesty, *Sah*. It's my unpleasant duty to report a crime."

Vince was agog.

The King lifted his feet for the footman to sweep underneath. "What crime?"

9

"Kidnap, *Sah*!"

"Wow!" said Vince.

"Quiet, boy," the King said. "This is important. Who's been kidnapped, Boxer?"

"*Sah*! Regimental mascot, *Sah*!"

Vince snorted. "Someone's actually stolen Mucky Bucky?"

Boxer turned a mean eye on the Prince. "Yes, Yer 'ighness. Some - *swine* - has kidnapped Buckingham Braithwaite the Seventh."

The King unfolded his paper. "It's only a goat, Boxer. Sort it out, there's a good chap."

Vince saw his chance. "I'll sort it out, Dad," he said. "Go on, let me. I'll detect the kidnapper."

The King shrugged. "Do what you like. Anything for a quiet life."

Vince was thrilled. "You mean it? I can really do something important? Promise, Dad?"

The King rustled his newspaper impatiently. "I said so, didn't I?"

Captain Boxer was agitated. "Beg pardon, Yer Majesty, it's more serious than that. The

Curse, Yer Majesty, *Sah!*"

The King fidgeted. "Um. Curse. Yes."

"What curse?" Vince looked from one to the other.

In a mournful voice, the Captain recited:

> "If the goat be away
> Three night and three day
> Guardsmen take heed
> You'll soon all be deed."

"Deed?" said the Prince.

"It means dead, Yer 'ighness, only it didn't rhyme."

The King burst out, "Superstitious nonsense. Pay the ransom and be done with it."

"No ransom note yet. *Sah!*"

"No need to pay it then." The King hid behind his paper.

Vince took Boxer into the corridor, to the Queen's obvious relief. "I'll get Mucky Bucky back for you, Captain."

"I hope so, Yer 'ighness." Boxer mopped his forehead with a regimental hanky. "If you don't, then as from Saturday morning, the men will stop being guardsmen for fear of their lives." He swallowed. "And that meansæ"

"What?" Vince whispered.

"For the first time in history, Yer 'ighness, this here castle, this stronghold, this Royal home, will be unguarded."

"Corks!" said the Prince. "I'd better get detecting.'

2

SOME DISGUISE!

Vince, beginning at the scene of the crime, found the guardsmen nervous and downcast. Boxer showed him a large airy stable, labelled "Honorary Guardsman Buckingham Braithwaite 2nd 3rd 4th 5th 6th 7th". It was spotless, except for the floor which was strewn with straw, damp in patches.

"It's quite clean," Vince said, surprised. "How come the goat's so mucky and smelly?"

"Rolls about a lot, Yer 'ighness."

Vince knew detectives searched for clues and evidence, but there was only the straw to examine. He didn't fancy poking through that.

So he interrogated Boxer instead. "What time was the kidnap?"

"Early morning, Sah. His little bed was still 'ot and steamy when we found 'im gorn."

"Where is his bed?"

"Standing in it, Yer 'ighness."

Vince stepped back smartly, but lost his footing. The Captain helped him up and was about to brush him down, when he saw the state of the Prince's rear end. "You need special detecting clothes, Yer 'ighness," he suggested, nose higher than ever.

Vince washed and changed, then made his way down, down to the castle kitchen. Mrs Doughboy, the cook, had worked there all his life; he could talk to her, about anything.

"Hallo, Prince Vincent, lovey." She gave him a floury hug.

"It's quiet in here, Mrs D."

"Young Larky's out pulling carrots, that's why," said the cook. "What you been up to, lovey?"

Proudly, Vince told her he had a real job at last.

"That's good," said Mrs Doughboy. "You might wait for ever to be King, and you can't do nothing that long." She patted pastry into a pie dish. "Going to be a detective, eh?"

Between bites of spicy sausage, Vince explained that he needed special detecting clothes, so everyone would know what he was.

Mrs Doughboy thought a moment. "Remember the Junior Detective Kit you had when you were a littl'un?"

Vince nodded. "Yes! The Mighty Magnifying Glass and the Crackproof Code Book would do, and the Snooper's Hat, but the Sleuth's Raincoat would be too small. Don't suppose they make a Senior Detective Kit." He looked down at his legs. "Not long enough for me."

Mrs Doughboy winked. "Run and find the Kit, Prince lovey. I'll sort you out a raincoat. A detective has to have a raincoat, to look the part."

Vince searched the Royal Toy Room, found his Junior Detective Kit and put on the tartan Snooper's Hat. It had ear flaps that you could wear turned up or down.

He changed into trainers, for silent prowling. Vince was only supposed to wear trainers for tennis; being Royal, the King insisted he dressed royally - shined shoes and no jeans.

Mrs Doughboy, sitting sewing by the kitchen range, didn't hear him return because the kitchen maid had just come in, singing a raucous song. "*Ooooh I love my little cockatoo, He sings so sweet, He sings so true,* here y'are." Carrots crashed, one by one, into a tin bowl.

"Be quiet, Larky!" Mrs Doughboy bellowed. "You're all bang, clatter, squawk!"

Larky curtsied to Vince. "Morning, Highness, that's a - unusual hat."

19

Mrs Doughboy
turned.
"Hello, lovey.
You found it, then?
Those flaps
will keep
your ears
cosy, won't
they?
I'm nearly done." She stitched swiftly. "My
hubby's old raincoat. It was far too short, so I
chopped a lump off the one the gardener put
out for the scarecrow and joined it on." She
bit the thread and held up the raincoat.
"There. Plenty long enough."

It was. As Larky said, it would keep his
ankles warm. "Can I go with you, Highness?"
she shrilled when she heard what he was up to.
"Mucky Bucky knows me. I take him kitchen
scraps. And I know an old goat-herding song
that might help us find him."

"No thanks, Larky." Vince put on dark
glasses and drew himself up. "This case won't
be difficult to crack."

Mrs Doughboy smiled fondly. "Talks like a real private eye, don't he?"

Feeling sharp-eyed and clever, Vince set off. "Which way?" he muttered at the castle gates. "Better just follow my nose."

After all, he thought, what better way to find the smelliest goat in the land than to follow his nose?

3
A CLUE, CHEWED

Vince headed for the post office. News always reached there first.

The postmistress had a coughing fit when he came in. "Sorry, Your Highness," she said, when she recovered.

"How did you recognise me?"

"By, er - your royal bearing." She coughed again. "Unmistakably our Prince."

That gave Vince a lovely warm feeling, and he didn't mind being recognised at all. People would know he was on Official Business because of his detective outfit.

"The regimental goat has been kidnapped," he said briskly. "Heard anything?"

The queue that had formed behind Vince melted away and the postmistress shifted uncomfortably. "Like what, Your Highness?"

"Um, kidnappers whispering in corners. Bleats in the night. Things like that."

The postmistress busied herself with a rubber stamp. Thump, thump. "Can't say I have, Your Highness," she said. Thump, thump.

It was the same everywhere. Nobody had heard anything. Nobody had seen anything. In fact, nobody seemed the slightest bit interested, even when he quoted the Curse.

A crowd of children leaving school recognised him. "It's Prince Vincent! Hi, Prince Vince!"

"You saw through my disguise!"

"Why *are* you disguised?" asked Carolina Boon, the oldest.

"I've been appointed Royal Detective," Vince said, embroidering on that morning's discussion with the King. "My first case is the kidnapping of the regimental goat."

It happened again.

The children bowed, said goodbye, and slunk away.

In seconds, Vince was alone.
What *was* going on?

Dinner that evening was ghastly. The King, eyes twinkling, asked how the mighty detective was shaping up.

"OK." Vince took a parsnip from the dish Macclesfield offered.

Three of the butler's fingers were sticking-plastered.

"I'm reading a detective story now." The Queen propped her book against the water jug. "If you want any pointers you can... " She tailed off, already engrossed in the story.

"Can what?" Vince asked, partly to annoy her and partly to keep the heat off himself.

"Never mind."

The King rubbed his hands together. "What progress in this ridiculous state of affairs? Curse. Hah!"

"Captain Boxer's men take it seriously," said Vince. "The castle won't be guarded from Saturday onwards. Anyone could walk in."

"Pah! Who'd dare?" The King attacked an over-crispy roast potato, shooting half to the floor. "What progress, I asked?"

"Nmn."

"Say again?"

"None."

The King poked his tongue into his cheek. It was his I-told-you-so look.

I'll show them, Vince fumed, as Macclesfield carefully sliced chocolate gateau.

A footman announced Captain Boxer.

"Beg pardon for distarbin' the Royal pudding, Yer Majes*ties,* but I discovered a clue in Buckingham's little bed."

Vince shuddered.

"And," Boxer continued, "I've brought it for the Prince Detective."

Vince glanced triumphantly at the King. "Bring it here, Captain, please."

Boxer, who hadn't learned from the events at breakfast, advanced, nose high, unaware of half a roast potato in his path. This time he stayed upright, but slid towards Vince, banging his tummy on the table and toppling the water jug.

The Queen screeched as iced water flowed over the book into her lap. Macclesfield grabbed a cloth, receiving a stinging jab from the corkscrew, which was underneath.

29

Vince took advantage of the chaos and left, clutching his first real clue - a well-chewed pencil.

He examined it on the way upstairs. If the goat had chewed it, the pencil would be bitten all over, instead of at one end. No, this reminded Vince of what he used to do during lessons. One end between the teeth, and gnaw.

This was a schoolchild's pencil.

4

TOUGH TOAD

Vince timed his visit for school lunch break.
He asked a boy reading comics in a corner of
the playground, "Where's Carolina Boon?"

"Doing something." The boy's eyes shot
everywhere. "For Miss Toadwell."

"Who's she? Where's Miss Smith?"

"Gone to look after her sister, so we've got
Miss Toadwell till she gets back. It should have
been someone else, but he couldn't come and
we thought we wouldn't have a teacher. Then
Miss Toadwell turned up."

"I'll go and see her," Vince said.

The boy laughed dryly. "Good luck. She's tough."

"What do you mean?"

"What I said. Tough Toad, we call her."

Vince found Miss Toadwell at her desk, eating treacle tart. She was a big woman - not tall, but big. Her dress was patterned with blue roses, big as cabbages, and a hairy brown cardigan was draped round square shoulders.

Her eyebrows lifted over a blunt red nose. "Yes?"

Vince introduced himself as Vincent Alexander, Detective. "I'm investigating a kidnapping."

"Goatnapping," Miss Toadwell corrected him. "If it were a baby goat it *would* be kidnapping, but as it's a full-grown one, it should be goatnapping. How can I help you?"

Vince wasn't sure about the goatnapping, but he wondered how Miss Toadwell knew so much. *He* hadn't mentioned a goat.

She licked a finger and dabbed at crumbs sprinkled over a large drawing on her desk.

More a plan than a drawing, Vince thought.
"That looks interesting," he said. "What is it?"

Miss Toadwell became flustered. "I'm
designing a house." She leaned forward,
smothering the drawing with an expanse of
blue roses, but not before Vince spotted the
words 'stable block'.

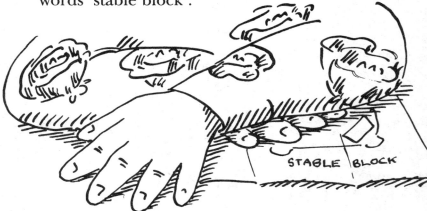

STABLE BLOCK

"Seems a very grand house," he remarked.
"Almost a castle."

Instantly, Miss Toadwell turned the plan
over. "I'm sorry I can't help with your
investigation. Good day."

She clearly didn't intend to say anything
more, so Vince apologised for interrupting
her lunch, and left.

Something odd was going on.

At four o'clock, he cornered the boy he'd spoken to earlier and showed him the pencil. "Any idea whose this is?"

"Carolina Boon's," the boy said promptly. "Hers are all like that." He held out his hand. "I'll give it back."

"Not so fast," said Vince. "You're all up to something, and it's to do with Mucky Bucky."

The boy reddened, biting his lip.

"Tell me," said Vince. "But don't lie," he added, as the boy opened his mouth. "I can spot lies with my eyes shut."

The boy blinked. "It's not for money," he said. "We don't want money. We want the King to change the laws - the stupid ones. Miss Toadwell said if we take the goat he'll listen to us. She knows how to get things done, my mum says."

"I thought so!" Vince was elated. "She"

"She'll be out for her walk in a minute! I'm off."

"Wait! Where does she go?"

"Over there, for miles." The boy waved towards the castle. "Sorry, Prince, I'm not being seen talking to you - she's coming!" He fled.

Vince hid behind a lamppost and watched Miss Toadwell stump across the road to a field gate. She perched on the bottom rail and hoisted over first one short leg, then the other. When she'd disappeared, Vince crossed to peer through the hedge. Miss Toadwell was crouched in the middle of the field, looking through binoculars.

She was spying on the castle!

Vince was certain the drawing was somehow connected to all of this. If Miss Toadwell was checking out the castle, she'd be away for a while and there'd be enough time to find out for sure. He raced to the schoolhouse. The drawing was still on her desk, rolled in a rubber band. His hands fumbled and the band snapped as he yanked it off. He flattened the paper.

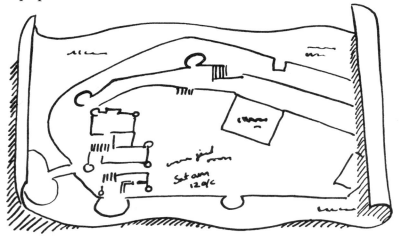

It *was* a plan. A plan of the castle. Noticing a red ring around one room, Vince examined the tiny lettering. It said 'Crown Jewel Room' and 'Sat. a.m. 12 o/c'.

The Queen's Official Birthday Garden Party was to be held on Saturday morning. It was also when the guards would cease duty.

He started at the clump of heavy footsteps. Corks! Miss Toadwell!

He mustn't be caught trespassing! Vince dived for the only other door, and hurled himself into the school store room.

Just in time, he realised there was no handle on the inside, and grabbed a book from one of the piles stacked against the wall. He dropped the book in the doorway. Now it couldn't close and lock him in.

Through the gap he watched Miss Toadwell, at her desk, pick up the rubber band, frowning. It dangled limply. Thank goodness he'd broken it. She'd think it had snapped, letting the paper unroll.

Miss Toadwell scooped up the plan and passed from Vince's view. He heard her tut-tut. Next moment her square-toed shoe appeared in the gap left by the open door. With a swift kick, she sent the book skittering across the store room floor. The door slammed.

Vince was trapped.

5

Alarm Bells

Vince breathed deeply to steady his nerves, then fumbled over the walls, feeling for a light switch. He went weak with relief when he found one and the room was lit by a dusty orange bulb.

Now what? Vince was in a proper fix. No food, no water and no fresh air. He squinted at a peeling notice on the door.

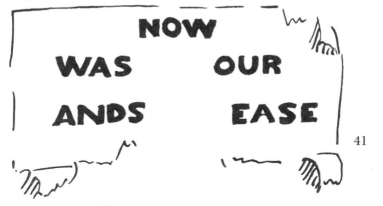

NOW

WAS   OUR

ANDS   EASE

41

It made no sense until he realised it was partly torn away. It should have read 'NOW WASH YOUR HANDS PLEASE'. This room must once have been the children's toilets.

Vince peeled off his raincoat and turned his ear flaps up. It was warm. He hoped it wouldn't get too warm. If only there was a window.

Something scratched at his mind. What was it?

Of course! If this had been toilets, there must be a window. Vince scrabbled at the book stacks, sending them tumbling to the floor.

It was there. High up, and small, but it *was* a window!

He tugged vainly at the rusty catch. It wouldn't budge. He'd have to break the glass. Suppose Miss Toadwell heard?

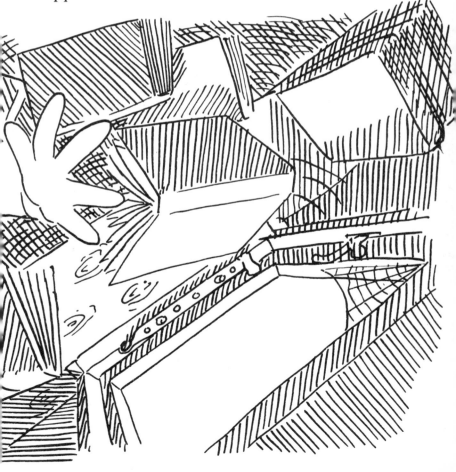

Vince searched the shelves and found a roll of sticky tape. He stuck strips across the window in a star shape, then used his magnifying glass to smash it. The splinters, held together by tape, scarcely tinkled, and it was a few seconds work to pull them away.

Vince laid his coat over the sill for protection and heaved himself through, glad for once that he was so thin. Outside, he leaned against the wall gathering his thoughts.

This had nothing to do with changing the laws. That was all a pretence; a smoke-screen. Miss Toadwell was planning to steal the Crown Jewels. She'd masterminded the kidnapping - *goat*napping, Vince thought angrily - so the castle would be unguarded, waiting to be robbed.

Well, not if he had anything to do with it. Vince pulled his ear flaps down and hurried to the church, where he hauled on the great bell rope. **CLANG! CLANG! CLANG!**

The villagers hastened to the church in

response to the traditional alarm signal. Vince counted on Miss Toadwell, a newcomer, not knowing it *was* an alarm. He hoped she was far enough away not to hear it at all.

As the chimes died away, Vince climbed on a chair to address the crowd. "I may look like an ordinary detective," he said, "but underneath this disguise," - he removed the glasses and turned up his ear flaps - "underneath, I am Vincent Alexandro de Maximus Roy. Your Prince!"

"We know," a quiet voice said.

Vince hid his disappointment. "I'm here to tell you you're committing a crime."

"Only crime I'm committing is burning my spuds," said a woman.

Vince ignored her. "*Why* did you kidnap the regimental mascot?"

Everyone spoke at once. He turned his back and pulled his flaps down, determined to ignore them until they shut up. But if he wasn't listening, they weren't staying. "Stop!" he yelled, realising they were leaving. "Please listen!"

46

"That's what we want you to do, Your Highness," said the postmistress.

"OK, I'm listening."

Out it poured. "Most of our young people have to leave the village to find work," said the postmistress. "That's Footman's Law."

Vince knew that one. It dated from when his great-great-great-grandfather's second footman, a villager, stole the King's boots. The whole village was punished by a law banning them from working at the castle. Only family of present or previous staff might work there.

"The village has been punished enough," said the postmistress. "Footman's Law's outdated."

"So's the one about the guardsmen being two metres tall in boots and busbies," said Carolina's dad. "Plenty of our lads would make better guards than that namby-pamby lot, all ruled by a goat. They just aren't tall."

"Sorry, Your Highness," said the postmistress, "but the King's old-fashioned. He hates change."

Vince wouldn't argue with that. "But what can he do if you don't tell him what you want?"

Carolina's dad seethed, "Come off it, Your Highness. He *knows* what we want, from Miss Toadwell's ransom note."

There were angry shouts. "He doesn't care."

"He's old-fashioned."

"*And* stuck-in-the-mud."

"Down with the King!"

Vince tried to calm the yelling mob before they turned nasty. Just as he feared he might be set upon, a voice cut across the clamour like a jet drowning the buzz of bees.

"*Shut* UP, *you lot!*"

Tongues stilled, every face turned towards

the door.

Only one person had a voice that piercing, that loud, that shattering. Larky - out walking her shaggy little dog, Goofer. "Go on, Highness," she said into the stunned silence. "You was saying?"

"I said no ransom note was delivered."

There was a puzzled hum.

"But Miss Toadwell sent it," said Carolina Boon's dad. "There's some mistake. I'll go and talk to her."

"Why *her?*" Vince demanded.

"Because she's helping us."

"Helping you?" Vince nearly exploded. "She's *using* you - to rob the King!"

The villagers listened, flabbergasted, as Vince told them about Miss Toadwell's plan of the castle, and what was written on it.

"She can't be a criminal," an elderly man protested. "She's a *schoolteacher*."

Vince raised one eyebrow. "She isn't the teacher Miss Smith said was coming, is she? You were expecting someone else. Mysterious, isn't it?"

A momentary silence was followed by a lot of muttering and quite a few arguments as people tried to work out what was going on. Eventually they all agreed that Miss Toadwell was definitely up to no good.

Carolina Boon's dad spoke for them. "We'll return Mucky Bucky and have nothing more to do with that woman," he announced.

Everyone muttered in agreement, but Vince stopped them. "We must let her think her plot's still working," he said. "Then we'll catch her. Red-handed!"

That caused plenty of excitement, but Vince scarely heard, even when people came up to congratulate him. He wanted to save the Crown Jewels, of course. But more importantly - his parents would see what he was capable of.

He'd show them!

A Buggling
Brainwave

Mrs Boon nearly fainted when Carolina
invited the Prince to tea and half the village
crammed themselves into her front room.

"Where *is* the goat?" Vince asked.

"In my garden shed, Your Highness," Mrs
Boon replied. "I'll show you while the kettle's
boiling."

She grumbled about Mucky Bucky all the
way down the path. "I've had compost heaps
aplenty," she said, "but this animal pongs fit to
beat the lot. I walked him round a bit today
and what did he do to the rhubarb patch?

He rolled in it, that's what he did, all over my lovely fresh, steaming manure."

The top half of the shed door was open, letting the evening sunshine in. As Vince looked inside Mucky Bucky jumped up to look outside. There was a clash of heads. Mrs Boon fished a clump of tissues from her pocket and gave them to Vince to staunch the blood.

"It's squashed by doze!"

"Don't talk, Highness. You need a cup of tea."

Vince stuffed wads of tissue into each nostril and followed Mrs Boon.

Larky and Carolina had made tea and
everyone balanced cups and cheese
sandwiches on their knees. There weren't
enough plates, so Vince had to use a table
mat. Goofer snaked between people's legs,
cleaning up crumbs.

As they ate, Vince revealed his plan. "I'll
buggle the goat."

54

"How do you buggle a goat?" a boy asked.

Larky giggled, making the man next to her spill his tea. "He means 'smuggle'."

Vince pressed on, "I'll buggle the goat idto the castle grouds udder cover of by bum's garden party. Thed I'll lie id wait add watch Biss Toadwell bake her way idside."

There were excited shivers, and several plates wobbled off shuddering knees.

"Dext," Vince said, "I'll alert the guards."

"But the Curse," said Carolina Boon. "They won't work if they think the goat's missing."

"I'll *show* theb the goat," said Vince, "thed they'll arrest the Toad." He rose to leave, followed by Larky and Goofer.

Everybody stood, shooting crusts and teaspoons to the floor and the last thing Vince heard was Mrs Boon saying, "*Look* at that carpet. Princes and goats, I don't know which is worse."

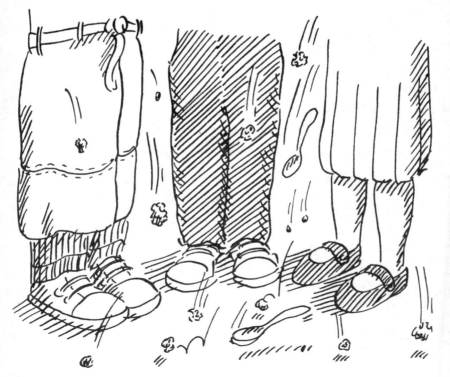

Larky chattered shrilly as they walked, so Vince didn't hear the schoolchildren tearing along behind them, shouting, "Prince Vince! Wait!"

"We did the kidnapping," Carolina panted, "and we've been feeding the goat and cleaning it - well, trying to - so can't we watch what happens?"

"Please!" the others begged.

Vince promised to find a way and went in search of the Queen, thinking hard.

She was in the bath. He banged on the door. "Bum!"

Silence, then a menacing, "*What* did you say?"

Vince pulled the tissue plugs from his nose. "I said Mum."

"What?" she snapped. "I'm reading."

Surprise, surprise, Vince thought. "Mum, what entertainment are you having for the garden party?"

"I'm not," came the cross reply. "I *was* having the regimental marching band, but apparently they're not working on Saturday. I don't know, who's ruling the country?"

"Mum."

"*What?*"

"What's it called when people dress up and make a scene from history or a book, and they keep dead still and everyone claps?"

"A tableau, and we don't want any of those. They're old-fashioned - we'd be bored stiff. Stiffer than usual."

"I've got an idea, Mum," Vince called.

"WHAT?! I'm *reading*."

"What about a moving and speaking tableau?"

"It's too late to organise it for Saturday."

Vince put his mouth to the door. "I'll organise one."

"You?" The Queen sniffed. "Huh!"

Vince wheedled, "Go on, let me."

"What? Oh, all *right*. Go away."

There was a small splash.

"*Look* what you've made me do, you chump! I've nothing to read now."

But Vince had gone.

7

"GET BACK!"

Early on Saturday Vince, wearing his detective outfit and carrying a holdall and shepherd's crook, asked Mrs Doughboy if he could borrow Larky.

She didn't mind; the party food was ready. "There's my centrepiece, Prince lovey," she said, proudly. "Castle Pudding!"

Vince gazed in admiration.

"Chocolate *out*side," Mrs Doughboy said. "Jelly and cream *in*side. It's a mite wobbly, so Larky's best out of the way for a bit."

Goofer ambled in and sniffed the Castle Pudding, soaring above him. Larky's braying voice followed. "*Razzle, dazzle, I'm in a frazzle, Keep me cool with a . . .*"

Mrs Doughboy bustled to the door. "Hush up, Larky. Mind my pud."

Vince picked up his crook. "Get my bag, Larky."

She heaved at the holdall. "Where we going?" Her whisper sounded like a hedge cutter.

Mrs Doughboy shooed her out. "Back by eleven, mind."

61

In the woods just outside the gates, Vince hid the holdall in a rhododendron bush. On the way to the Boons' house, he told Larky, "We'll get Mucky Bucky and smuggle him into the castle. The Toad mustn't see us." He glanced at Larky's excited face. "Or hear us."

She laughed, making him wince. "I *can* be quiet. So can Goofer. And Mucky Bucky likes him, so that should help."

Carolina answered the door and let them into the back garden. "Mum and Dad's out," she said, "so leave by the side gate. I'm off to collect the other kids. Where shall we meet?"

"In the woods by the castle gates," said Vince.

Goofer sniffed and shot down the path. They found him jumping at the shed door. The goat bleated gently.

Mucky Bucky was really quite revolting. His white coat was grubby and matted with goodness-knows-what. One horn was smeared with sticky yellow goo, and half a jam tart clung to his underneath.

Vince slipped his raincoat belt through Mucky Bucky's collar before daring to open the door. When he did, the goat charged out to Goofer, and the jubilant animals dashed across the garden with Vince desperately hanging on. They stopped in the petunia patch and jigged round each other, bleating and barking, then bolted straight for Mrs Boon's ornamental fish pond.

Vince scarcely knew what was happening.

One minute he was squidging through the strawberry bed, the next he was up to his knees in goldfish and water weed.

On they raced across the grass, the goat pausing only to grab a tea towel from the washing line. If it hadn't been for the tall side gate, they might never have stopped. Vince caught his breath as Mucky Bucky destroyed the tea towel and Goofer demolished the jam tart.

Larky was helpless with laughter. "Cor, you look a sight, Your Highness," she hooted, wiping her eyes.

"Sh!" Vince unlatched the gate and peeped out. "All clear." He opened it wide.

There was no warning. Suddenly, the gateway was completely blocked by a menacing figure.

"Not quite clear," smirked the Toad.

Vince and Larky froze. Goofer sniffed Miss Toadwell's feet. She pushed him away, none too gently, with her toe. "Sit!"

He sat.

The Toad swept Goofer into her arms and bore down on them. "Back you go. Back!"

Vince felt Larky's fury. "It'll be OK," he whispered. "Help me with Mucky Bucky."

"Keep going," growled the Toad and, as she loomed over them, they edged back, never taking their eyes from the threatening face.

"Put my dog down," Larky shrieked hoarsely.

"Back, I said."

Larky bravely stood her ground.

Tough Toad gripped the trembling Goofer's throat. "Wouldn't want me to hurt the dear doggie, would you?" she sneered.

Larky gulped, and moved back with Vince, all the way to the shed. The Toad opened the door. "In."

"In there?" Vince was aghast. "The goat's been in there."

"And he's going back." The Toad pushed them in, Mucky Bucky too, and shut the bottom half of the door. Then, to Vince and Larky's horror, she slammed the top shut. "*Now* try and get the better of me - Mister Detective." The bolt scraped home.

They were imprisoned, with a cantankerous goat, in the appallingly smelly dark. Vince covered his mouth and nose with his hands. "No window this time," he muttered.

"My poor Goofer," Larky groaned.

"Quiet!" Vince tilted his head, listening.

"What is it?" Larky's voice trembled. "What's out there?"

8 PRINCE BO~PEEP

Vince pressed his ear against the rough shed door. He heard Goofer bark furiously, closely followed by a roar from the Toad. "Mangy brute!" she shouted. "Get away from me. *Get!*"

The gate slammed.

"She's gone," said Vince. "I think she's left Goofer behind. This is our chance, but there's not much time. The party'll be starting soon." He listened at the door again. "Call Goofer, Larky," he urged. "Quick - top of your voice."

He held his ear flaps down firmly as Larky filled her lungs and bawled, "Goooo-fer! *Gooooo-fer!* GOOFER COME 'ERE YOU LITTLE DEVIL YOU!"

Mucky Bucky stiffened at the noise, then twitched his ears, listening. Goofer's joyful barks grew louder as he neared the shed.

Vince kept an eye on the goat. "Stand back, Larky," he warned.

Mucky Bucky pushed at the door. He backed off, then charged, butting it with his rock-hard forehead.

Larky got the idea. "*Gooofer-oofer-oofer!*" she bellowed.

The door splintered as Mucky Bucky lashed
out with his hooves. He charged again and
again, until the bottom half of the shed door
shattered. Once more, and he smashed
through. Vince and Larky screwed up their
courage and their noses before kneeling in the
soggy, smelly straw and crawling into cool fresh
air.

Mucky Bucky and Goofer were busy
nuzzling each other, so Vince and Larky
caught them easily.

"Hurry." Vince opened the gate, even more cautiously. "We must get through the village without Toad spotting us."

Larky noticed six cows grazing in Farmer Bird's field. "That's what we need." She sprinted across the road, rounded up the cows and herded them towards the Boons' gate. "Get in the middle as we come past," she called.

Vince crouched with his legs splayed out and ran like a great crab between the cows' hot flanks, pulling Mucky Bucky with him. Larky kept low on the side away from the schoolhouse and herded cows, dog, goat and Prince through the village towards the castle, where they veered off into the woods.

"If the Toad was watching," Vince said, "she couldn't have seen us. You can take the cows back to Farmer Bird's now."

Larky kicked a pine cone. "Sorry, Highness. Mrs Doughboy said I'm to be back by eleven."

Vince thought. "No matter. There's a field just through those trees." He pointed. "They'll be safe there for now."

Larky took the cows to the field, then returned to work, whispering a noisy, "Good luck". Vince tethered Mucky Bucky to a tree and, within moments, saw the children running through the woods.

"We've been searching for you," said Carolina Boon. She sniffed. "Pyaugh! What's that?"

"Sorry." Vince made a face. "It's me. Look, the party's started. We must get going, but you'll have to wait while I sneak into the guardhouse."

He'd been worried about doing this, but the men had been so busy packing they didn't notice the stranger in the long raincoat and tartan hat who disappeared into the tack room.

Vince helped himself to the horses' ceremonial sheepskin rugs and staggered back with them to the children. "Put one of these on and be a sheep." He retrieved his holdall, took out some string and tied two sheepskins round Mucky Bucky. Carolina pulled ropes of ivy from a tree and twisted them round the goat's horns. "You can't tell what he is now," she said. "What about you, Your Highness? You're too long for a sheep."

Vince removed his hat and raincoat, and produced a long frilly blue dress and footman's wig from the holdall. He put them on over his own clothes and picked up the shepherd's crook. "Well?"

The sheepskinned children fell about laughing.

"Lovely, Princess," said one.

"Stupid girl," Vince said. "I'm Little Bo-peep."

There was more hysterical laughter. "*Big Bo-peep!*"

"You should practise baaing instead of making that racket," Vince said peevishly. "If the Queen realises what's happening she'll tell the King and he'll have you all turned into lamb chops."

That silenced them. Vince held tight to Mucky Bucky and led his flock through the castle gate, unchallenged by the guards.

As they neared the garden party, he recited in a clear voice, "Little Bo-peep has lost her sheep."

"Baa," bleated the "sheep". "Baa, baa."

"And doesn't know where. . . "

The Queen, looking utterly bewildered, hurried across. "What do you look like? What *do* you think you're doing?"

Vince straightened his wig. "It's my moving tableau," he said. "We're entertaining the guests."

"Don't be ridiculous," said the Queen. "I've *got* an entertainer - Knifo the Sword Swallower. Can't you see?"

Vince realised the guests were ignoring him and his flock; instead they were gasping at Knifo in his black hood and shiny red cloak. "Where did he come from?"

"I don't know," the Queen said impatiently, "but I'm jolly glad he did. He's topnotch." She looked Vince up and down. "*Do* get indoors

before anyone sees how ridiculous you look.
You're lucky your father's late as usual. I don't
know what he'd say."

Vince took his subdued flock around the side of the castle. Once out of sight of the Queen, they tore through the orchard and deposited Mucky Bucky in an empty pig sty before stripping him of his disguise.

"Aren't you going to show the guards we've brought the goat back?" Carolina Boon asked.

"Later," said Vince. If he took Mucky Bucky back too soon, the men would go back on guard duty and Miss Toadwell wouldn't be able to get near the Crown Jewels. And if she didn't try to steal the Jewels, Vince couldn't save them and catch her red-handed.

The children shook themselves out of their sheepskins, enjoying the cool breeze, but they froze at an ear-piercing, "Hey - you lot!"

It was only Larky, bringing food and water for Mucky Bucky. The children watched thirstily as he sat in the food to drink from the pail she held for him.

Larky laughed, making the goat jump. "Mrs Doughboy says you're all to come in for a drink."

The children looked imploringly at Vince.

"OK," he said, "but we must be lying in wait near the Crown Jewel room before twelve. We've got this far. We can't let Miss Toadwell get away with it." He reached down to the hem of his dress and pulled it up over his head.

"She's not there," said a boy.

Vince struggled to pull the dress clear of his ears. "What?"

"She's not at the garden party. I looked, when you were squabbling with your mum. You can't miss her, not Tough Toad. She wasn't there."

Vince gulped and rolled the dress into a ball. Surely he hadn't made a mistake - a dreadful mistake?

9

KNIFO

The only thing to do was stick to the plan so, just before midday, silent watchers littered the stairway above the Crown Jewel Room.

At one minute to twelve, heavy feet thonk-thonk-thonked up towards them.

The burglar? Surely not.

It wasn't. A familiar voice screeched through the stairwell. "Prince Vince? Look out the window, quick!"

"Thanks, Larky." Vince peered over the nearest windowsill.

"What is it?" Carolina hissed.

Vince sank back. "Only Knifo the Sword Swallower." He stopped. Wasn't there something strange about Knifo's movements? Sort of furtive? He had another look. Knifo was scurrying towards the castle. There was something familiar - that stocky shape, that rolling walk.

Miss Toadwell!

"No wonder we didn't spot her at the party," he said. "Miss Toadwell is a man - she's Knifo!" He hunched down on the stairs. "Remember, we want her - him - in the Crown Jewel room before we fetch the guards."

Hearts banging, they peeped through the banisters as Knifo, in black and swirling red, stole to the Crown Jewel Room, glanced round, and slipped inside.

"Larky, get Mucky Bucky," Vince ordered, "and bring him to the guard house. Hurry! Everybody else, run!"

Praying there were still some guards left, they raced through the gallery, down the middle stairway, out and along the drive. At the guard house, Vince yelled, "Help!"

A handful of men emerged.

"There's a burglar in the Crown Jewel Room *right now*, and if you're quick you'll catch him stealing - what's wrong? Why are you shaking your heads?"

"The Curse, Your Highness," said a guard. "We don't work here now, not since the goat's gone three night and three day, or we'd all be . . ."

"Deed. I know," said Vince, "but that's all over." Triumphantly he announced, "Mucky Bucky's back." He swept an arm out and pointed across the lawn.

The guards looked. "Don't think so, Your Highness. Sorry." They went inside.

Vince was stiff with frustration. "Where's Larky with the goat?"

"Here she is!" Carolina cried. "But there's no Mucky Bucky!"

Larky ran up, panting. "He's escaped!"

Vince looked at Carolina. "Are you thinking what I'm thinking?" She nodded. "We'll have to catch the Toad - Knifo, I should say, ourselves."

Vince told Larky to keep searching for Mucky Bucky, then he made Carolina keep the children well back while he crouched behind a lilac bush to wait.

At sight of a red flash against the grey castle wall, he ran bent double, from tree to tree. Now he was only twenty metres from Knifo, whose shrouded figure, bulkier than ever, skirted the garden party, making for the main drive.

If Vince was to cut off Knifo's escape, he had to get between him and the gates. He ran to an oak tree.

Suddenly, Knifo turned. "You!"

Vince drew himself up. "Yes, I."

"Get out!" Knifo snarled. "This is Royal ground."

"And I," Vince replied, haughtily, "am Prince Vincent Alexandro de Maximus Roy, Official Royal Detective."

"Royal Detective, *poo!*" As Knifo reached under his cloak, a ripple of diamonds slithered to his feet.

The Queen's necklace! Now Vince knew where the Crown Jewels were. No wonder Knifo looked so huge.

Vince's attention snapped back as, with a flourish, Knifo brandished a gleaming silver sword.

The Queen and her guests hurried to see what was happening, but drew back, gasping, when they saw the weapon.

Vince's mouth had dried but he stood as steady as the nearby oak.

Knifo advanced, sword blazing in the sunlight.

"Don't be afraid, Vincent," the Queen called. "Knifo doesn't really swallow swords - it's an act. They're trick ones."

Knifo glanced back and laughed - a rolling, evil laugh. "Not all of them, dear Queen. Watch!" He darted to a flower-bed where blue delphiniums stood shoulder height above orange marigolds. The blade slashed once; five rich blue flower heads tumbled down, a nd Knifo laughed his villainous laugh. "Trick sword, eh?'

10 SURPRISE FOR THE KING

Vince's mouth felt full of sand. He was glad of the raincoat; at least no one could see his legs shaking.

Knifo circled sideways, his back to the castle, keeping the people in front where he could see them.

Vince noticed, over Knifo's left shoulder, a slight movement. Mucky Bucky was in the herb garden. Then another movement, to the right - Larky. He signalled frantically to her.

Knifo, thinking Vince was about to attack, thrust the sword point against his chest. "Don't try anything, Prince Detective," he sneered, "or it'll be the worse - for - you." On each of the final three words, he flicked the sword, neatly slicing off a raincoat button. Then he sidled to the right, towards the main drive.

Behind Knifo, Larky raced in a wide circle around Mucky Bucky. Vince could hear her singing the goat-herding song at the top of her horrible voice. He moved to block Knifo, provoking a fresh attack. This time the sword-point removed his hat.

"Yodel-odel-odel-o, Come my goat, 'tis time to go," Larky screeched. *"Yodel-odel-odel-i, The sun is sinking in the sky. Yodel-odel-odel-ee . . ."*

Mucky Bucky, understandably mad to escape that frightful racket, hurtled towards Knifo. He paused, stared straight at the red-cloaked figure, sniffed, and charged.

"Look out behind!" Vince yelled.

Knifo laughed scornfully. "I'm not falling for that."

Mucky Bucky was almost on him.

"Out of the way," Vince hollered.

Only when everyone else dived clear did Knifo glance behind.

In spite of his bulk, he moved quickly, crowns and swords clanking and red cloak flying. He made straight for the only thing that offered cover - the heavily-laden food table.

Mucky Bucky smelt his enemy. He picked up speed and, just as his quarry reached the table, butted him squarely in the bottom. Up Knifo sailed with a wild yell, and down, slap into the middle of the monstrous Castle Pudding.

There were screams of laughter. Guards appeared carrying suitcases, wondering what the rumpus was all about. They saw Knifo, freshly coated in lime jelly, chocolate and cream, slide slowly to the ground. They saw Mucky Bucky, grazing quietly on a plate of egg and cress sandwiches with a crown hooked over one horn. They saw the Prince point to Knifo.

"Guards," he announced, "the regimental goat is back, the Curse is lifted, and there's a burglar in the pudding. Arrest him!"

Knifo, laying new and colourful curses, was marched away between two escorts, to be handed over to Captain Boxer.

Macclesfield, bringing fresh tea, slid on the diamonds. Thud! Crash! He sat up, dazed. "What the... ?" Staggering to his feet, he pocketed the necklace, muttering something about there being a place for everything, and noticed the sword. "I'll remove that, Your Majesty," he told the Queen. "For safety's sake."

"Corks!" Vince flew to stop him. "I'll take it,

Macclesfield."

Too late.

"Done it again, Your Majesty," said the butler.

The Queen took a plaster from her pocket. "I thought you might."

Everyone was watching her patch up the butler when the King returned from his morning's fishing. "Having a good party, dear? Sorry I'm late. Any pudding left?"

The guests parted, revealing the mess, the Queen, Macclesfield, Mucky Bucky and, finally, his son in the most ridiculous hat he'd ever seen.

"What the dubbins is going on? And get that goat off the table."

The Queen began to explain, but realised she didn't know half the story and left it to Vince, Carolina Boon and Larky.

The King admitted they'd done a good job, and blushed to hear that the villagers thought him old-fashioned. He promised to change the laws immediately, especially Footman's Law - the one forbidding villagers to work in the castle.

"I can't find jobs for everybody," he said. "Even a King can only have so many bakers or court physicians. But," he continued, "when

your own teacher comes back, you children must study hard. Who knows, you might even become detectives." He reached up to clap Vince on the shoulder. "If he can do it, anyone can."

That hurt Vince's feelings. Larky saw his downcast face, drew breath, and bellowed right in the King's ear, "Three cheers for Prince Vince, the Royal Detective!"

The King and Queen stared, deafened and amazed, at the happy crowd cheering for *their* son. And Vince thought that they did look, just a little bit, proud.

I need a new case to solve, he thought, to prove this wasn't a fluke. I wish someone would report another crime.

Almost immediately, his wish came true. A large angry man in ancient wellies strode across the lawn towards them. "Are you the detective?"

Vince nodded.

"There's been a theft. Six of my best cows are missing. I want you to find them."

Six cows! Vince ignored Larky's giggles and pulled his ear flaps down. "No problem, Farmer Bird." He glanced at his father's astonished expression. "*No* problem for the Royal Detective!"